Join the Cutiecorns
on every adventure!

Heart of Gold

Purrfect Pranksters

Rainy Day Rescue

Cutiecorns

Rainy Day Rescue

by Shannon Penney
illustrated by Addy Rivera Sonda

SCHOLASTIC INC.

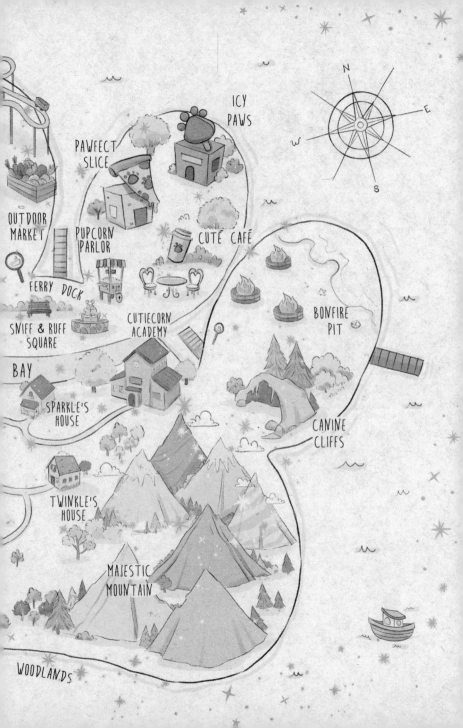

Text copyright © 2020 by Shannon Decker
Illustrations copyright © 2020 by Addy Rivera Sonda

ISBN 978-1-338-54043-7
10 9 8 7 6 5 4 3 2 1   20 21 22 23 24

Printed in the U.S.A. 40
First printing 2020

Book design by Jennifer Rinaldi

Scholastic Inc., 557 Broadway, New York, NY 10012
Scholastic UK Ltd., Euston House,
24 Eversholt Street, London NW1 1DB
Made in Jefferson City, U.S.A.

Chapter 1

"I've got it!" Glitter barked, racing across the sand. She skidded to a sudden stop, stood up on her back paws, and bopped the colorful beach ball with her nose. It sailed over the volleyball net and landed just behind her friend Sparkle.

"Bow wow! What a shot!" A little ball of fur appeared at Glitter's side, panting and

grinning. Flash was a Yorkshire Terrier with
boundless energy—the pawfect volleyball
partner!

Sparkle and Twinkle ducked under the net
to give Glitter high fives. "Not bad," Twinkle
said with a shrug. The Beagle was known for
being a little gruff and grumpy, but she was

always there for her friends. She winked at Glitter and gave her a little smile.

"At this rate, Twinkle and I are going to lose this game in the twitch of a tail," Sparkle woofed with a giggle. The afternoon sunshine reflected off the golden horn on Sparkle's head. It glimmered so brightly that Glitter had to shield her eyes with a paw!

"You're going to blind someone with that thing!" Flash joked.

Glitter couldn't help but laugh. It was a beautiful day with not a cloud in the sky, and Sparkle's horn *was* awfully bright in the sunlight! All of the pups had horns between their ears, each in a different color—Twinkle's was blue, Flash's was purple, and Glitter's was a beautiful pearly pink. They weren't ordinary puppies. They were Cutiecorns! Their horns gave them pawsome powers, which made their home, Puppypaw Island, a truly magical place to live.

"It's our serve," Glitter said, carrying the beach ball across the sand.

As she waited for her friends to get into place, Glitter took a deep breath of the salty sea air. Gentle waves lapped at the sand on one side of her, and grassy dunes rose on the other. A light breeze ruffled Glitter's white fur. She peered around the mostly empty beach, thinking about how lucky they were to call Puppypaw Island home.

Just then, something in the tall beach grass near the volleyball net caught her eye. She stopped and squinted through the sunshine.

Bow wow, it was a little French Bulldog! Glitter knew most of the pups on Puppypaw Island, but she had never seen this one before. He was mostly tan, so he blended into the sand, but he had a black muzzle and sweet black eyes. Two big ears stood tall on top of his head, with a royal-blue horn between them.

"Hi there!" Glitter called, waving a paw.

The pup looked around in alarm, clearly worried that he'd been spotted.

Glitter smiled and trotted over to him, leaving the beach ball behind. "I'm Glitter," she said with a friendly smile. "I'm sorry we didn't see you there sooner!"

The pup gave her a small smile in return. "I'm Batty," he said quietly. "I didn't mean to interrupt your game. It just looked like you were having so much fun! I had to stop and watch."

Glitter lowered her voice to a whisper. "We're having a pawsome time, but I think my friends Sparkle and Twinkle need some help. Would you like to play? They could really use you on their team!"

Batty blushed. "Really? I'm new here, and I've never played this game before."

"Well, this is a great way to learn!" Glitter said. "Where are you from?"

"My dad is a fisherpup, so we've traveled around a lot," Batty explained. "But now that I'm getting older, we're settling down in one spot. We just moved into a little house on the water." He pointed a paw down the beach.

Glitter beamed. "It's furbulous to meet you. Welcome to Puppypaw Island!" She turned and waved her friends over. "Guys, this is Batty. I thought he could join Sparkle and Twinkle's team, since they're struggling against the Puptastic Duo!"

"Hey!" Sparkle protested, laughing. She looked at Twinkle and shrugged. "We could probably use the help."

"Bark for yourself," Twinkle said, giving

Batty a sly wink. "But the more the merrier!"

Batty's face broke into a wide grin, and he jumped to his paws. "Ter-ruff-ic!" he cried, darting across the sand in excitement.

The older pups followed, heading back to their places on either side of the net. "That was really nice of you, Glitter," Flash whispered, nudging her friend. "He looks so happy!"

Glitter felt cozy inside as she picked up the beach ball. Caring magic was her specialty, so helping others came very naturally to her. She loved how a small gesture could turn someone's day from just okay to pawsitively grrrrreat!

"Here we go!" she barked, bopping the ball up and over the net with one paw. The pups hit it back and forth, back and forth, never letting the ball touch the sand. Finally, Batty took an enormous leap and knocked it over the net with his nose. Flash dove for it—but missed.

She rolled in the sand, laughing. "This can't be your first time playing, Batty. You're an expert!" she said.

Glitter held out a paw to help her up. Together, they watched Batty, Sparkle, and Twinkle cheer as they did a ridiculous victory dance.

"Okay, okay," Flash barked after a moment, giggling. "You guys have *one* point. Don't get your fur too ruffled yet—let's see if you can do it again!"

Chapter 2

When the sun started to sink lower in the sky, Glitter and her friends headed home for dinner. It had been a pawsome, sunny afternoon at the beach, and they were doggone hungry!

Glitter, Sparkle, Twinkle, and Flash all waved a paw at little Batty as he trotted home with a huge smile on his snout.

"I think Batty had a puptastic time,"

Sparkle barked as the four friends made their way up the twisty lane toward home. "And he totally saved our team!"

"It must be so hard moving to a new place," Glitter said thoughtfully. "I don't even like leaving you all at the end of the day. I can't imagine moving away for good!"

Flash tackled her in a big hug. "Don't worry, Glitter—you're stuck with us!"

Glitter felt warm and happy as she hugged Flash and Sparkle goodbye, then continued toward home with Twinkle. Her golden charm bracelet jingled as she walked. She'd gotten it at the Enchanted Jubilee, the ceremony that marked when pups were ready to begin using their magic. So far, her bracelet only had two charms on it—a Cutiecorn horn and a many-pointed star—but she'd be able to earn more as her magic skills grew. Barking bulldogs, she could hardly wait!

Glitter had been lost in her thoughts, but now she turned to Twinkle. "You're awfully quiet. Is everything okay?"

Twinkle scrunched up her snout. "I'm feeling a little nervous . . . about my magic."

Glitter stopped in her tracks. Woof, this was serious! She looked at her friend closely, and gave her time to bark on.

"Over the weekend, I made a mistake," Twinkle said quietly. "I was supposed to be watching my twin sister and brother at the playground. We were playing hide-and-seek, and I was using my seeing magic to track them down. It was too easy, so I told them to

spread out and hide farther away . . . but then I couldn't find them."

Glitter gasped. "That must have been so scary!"

"It was," Twinkle said. "I'd been feeling so confident. But when I couldn't find Tumble and Trot, I panicked and couldn't tap into my magic at all."

"So what did you do?" Glitter asked, giving Twinkle's paw a squeeze.

"I started barking up a storm!" Twinkle said. "I ran up and down the beach, woofing like a crazy pup, until they heard me and came out of hiding." She clapped a paw over her eyes. "Maybe I just shouldn't use my magic outside of school for now. It's too dangerous."

Glitter frowned. Twinkle was so pawsome at magic!

"You have some of the most ter-ruff-ic magic of any pup I know, Twinkle," she said gently. "But we're all still learning. Everyone makes mistakes!"

Twinkle shrugged, her snout hanging low.

"Okay, listen. I'm going to run up ahead and hide." Glitter gave her friend a big grin.

"And I want you to use your seeing magic to find me."

Twinkle's eyes grew wide, but Glitter held up a paw before she could bark a word. "You can do this, Twinkle. Just focus on your magic, and don't panic."

With that, Glitter turned on her paws and ran ahead. Once she'd gone around a bend, she ducked behind a bush bursting with fluffy white hydrangeas. Her fur blended right into the flowers, so she was almost impawsible to spot!

Moments later, she heard Twinkle trotting slowly up the road. Glitter held her breath, staying pawfectly still.

Time ticked by, and Glitter didn't hear anything. Was Twinkle still out there? Had she continued up the road? Oh no . . . had Glitter's plan backfired?

Slowly, so as not to make a sound, Glitter lifted her snout. Then she nearly jumped out of her fur—Twinkle was peeking down at her over the top of the bush!

"How long have you been there?" she yelped, bursting into giggles.

"For ages!" Twinkle could hardly bark because she was laughing so hard. "I can't believe you didn't see me looking down at you!"

Glitter swatted playfully at her friend. "See? Your magic is totally pawsome!"

Twinkle grinned. "Thanks, Glitter. I needed that!" She gave Glitter a big hug before racing home with a spring in her pawstep.

Glitter continued along with a smile stretched across her snout until her house came into view, a little cottage surrounded by bright flower beds. The yard was bursting with flowers of every color! A sweet smell wafted all around her. This was Glitter's favorite place in the whole world, paws down.

When she stepped through the door, familiar barks and woofs filled the air. Pans were banging in the kitchen. Someone was singing. Someone else went racing by in a blur of white fur. Life at Glitter's house was never boring! She had a whole pack of siblings: her brother Fizzle, sister Frolic, brother Pogo, and sweet baby Swirl. Glitter was the oldest of the bunch! They all had white fur, but each pup had a different-colored horn. Glitter's mom often said that, together, they created a whole rainbow!

"Glitter's home!" someone barked, and a little fluffball appeared at her side.

"Hi, Pogo," Glitter said, ruffling her youngest brother's soft fur. "Did you practice your

swimming today?" Pogo had always been scared of the water. Lately, Glitter had been using her caring magic to help him overcome his fears!

Pogo grinned proudly and stuck his snout into the air. "Mom took me and Swirl to the beach, and I doggy-paddled all by myself the whole time! It was pawsome!"

"Bow wow!" Glitter said. "I knew you could do it. You're turning into a puptastic swimmer!"

Pogo beamed as their dad's bark rang through the small cottage. "Dinnertime!"

"So how was everyone's day?" their mom asked as they all dug in.

"Frolic and I played pirates in Mistypaw Meadow this morning," Fizzle piped up. He was only a year younger than Glitter, and she knew he was excited to start using his magic soon.

"I met a new pup today," Glitter said softly. She wasn't the loudest in her house, but when she barked up, everyone listened.

"Really?" Frolic asked. "Where?"

"We were playing volleyball on the beach, and we invited him to join us," Glitter explained. She turned to Pogo. "His name is Batty. He's probably about your age."

Pogo howled with excitement. "Pawsome!"

Glitter had to smile at her brother's enthusiasm. "His dad is a fisherpup, and they just moved to Puppypaw Island. I think it must be hard for Batty, not knowing anyone here. Maybe you could keep an eye out for him around town, Pogo."

"Hot dog, you bet!" Pogo cried.

Glitter's dad gave her a wink. He was especially good at caring magic, just like her, and she knew he was proud of her for looking out for the new pup.

They all gobbled up their dinners, giggling as Frolic told a funny story about her friend accidentally falling in the fountain at Sniff and Ruff Square that afternoon. Bow wow! Glitter looked around the table. She had a full belly and was surrounded by the smiling snouts of her family. She was pawsitive that there was no place she'd rather be!

Chapter 3

"Okay, pups, gather around!" Mrs. Horne, the head of Cutiecorn Academy, clapped her paws for attention the next morning. Her turquoise horn sparkled in the morning sun streaming through the window.

Glitter, Flash, Sparkle, Twinkle, and the rest of their classmates formed a half circle in front of Mrs. Horne. Their barking died down immediately as they turned curious eyes on their teacher. Mrs. Horne always taught the most fascinating lessons, paws down!

"You've been at Cutiecorn Academy for a few weeks now, and you're all doing a doggone wonderful job so far," Mrs. Horne said kindly. "So today, we're going to try something new. Has anyone here ever felt like your magic was too big for you?"

The pups all looked around quizzically.

Flash's paw shot into the air. "I think so! The other day, I was using my magic to put toothpaste on my toothbrush. I don't know exactly what happened, but the tube of toothpaste exploded everywhere and my toothbrush flew out the window!"

Everyone burst out laughing.

"Grrrreat example—it sounds like your shifting magic got a little out of control, Flash," Mrs. Horne said, chuckling. "That's what we're going to work on today: controlling your magic. Sometimes you need your magic to be big, and sometimes you need it to be small."

Mrs. Horne divided the class of twelve pups

into pairs. Glitter was teamed up with Flash, who danced around and wagged her tail.

"Look out," Twinkle murmured to Glitter with a wink. "She's so excited, I wouldn't be surprised if her magic shifted you right out of the room, fur real! Don't forget what happened to that poor tube of toothpaste."

Glitter giggled and gave Twinkle an encouraging hug. It was pawsome to see her friend feeling happy and confident again!

Glitter and Flash moved to one corner of the room and worked on finding their magic. Thanks to their lessons, they'd gotten pretty good at locating their magic quickly! In no time, Glitter's pink horn and Flash's purple horn were shining brightly.

"Puptastic!" Mrs. Horne said, joining

them. "Now that you've both tapped into your magic, I want you to try intensifying it. Glitter, you first."

Glitter stood perfectly still, concentrating hard. The whole area around her filled with a warm pink glow as she felt her caring magic grow bigger and stronger. She focused in on Flash, sensing the magic extending from every piece of her fur.

"Now make your magic small again," Mrs. Horne instructed. "You can do it. You're in control."

Glitter squeezed her eyes shut. Hot dog, this part was harder! She hadn't practiced making her magic small before. Usually when she was done using her magic, she just stopped paying attention to it!

Slowly, slowly, Glitter was able to pull her magic back, until her horn only emitted the faintest gleam.

"What a furbulous job!" Mrs. Horne barked, clapping her paws. "Excellent control, Glitter."

Glitter beamed proudly, turning to Flash. "How did that feel to you?"

Flash leaped to her paws, dashing around her friend in a blur. "Pawsome!" she cried. "When your caring magic got bigger and stronger, it was like I was wrapped in a warm, soft blanket. I felt so safe and cozy. I was invincible, like a superpup! Do it again! Do it again!"

Mrs. Horne laughed. "How about you take a turn now, Flash?"

Flash stopped running at once. When it came to her magic, she was all business! She sat very still, facing Glitter.

"Nice and easy now," Mrs. Horne said quietly. "Glitter, are you ready?"

Glitter nodded. Flash had a lot of energy, but she was incredible at using her shifting magic. Glitter knew she was in good paws!

Flash's horn began to glow purple. Suddenly, Glitter felt herself sliding backward! She moved slowly at first, then a bit faster. Bow wow, it felt like she was gliding on an ice rink!

As Glitter reached the opposite side of the room, she felt herself slide to a gentle stop. A moment later, she was moving back toward Flash and Mrs. Horne!

When she reached them, she leaped into

the air. "Flash, that was pawfectly amazing!" she barked, throwing her paws around her friend. "I could tell you had your magic under control the whole time."

Flash danced around in triumph for a minute, then sat down in a heap. "You're the biggest thing I've ever moved with my magic. I'm doggone tired!" She laughed.

"Me too!" Glitter sat down next to her friend, and Flash's snout rested on her shoulder.

Mrs. Horne gave them a kind smile and a round of applause. "You've certainly earned a break. I'm proud of you both!" She moved along to work with some of the other pups.

Glitter sighed happily, watching as her classmates worked to control the size and intensity of their magic. "Ooh, it's Twinkle's turn—look!" she whispered to Flash.

But Flash didn't answer.

Glitter glanced down in surprise. Hot dog, Flash was fast asleep!

Chapter 4

"What a morning!" Flash barked as the pups headed to the school courtyard for lunch. "I'm hungry enough to eat a barge full of bones!"

Glitter put an arm around her friend. "You really worked up an appetite with that nap, huh?" she teased.

Glitter, Flash, Sparkle, and Twinkle set paw outside, breathing in the fresh air and soaking up the sun on their fur. Glitter noticed Sparkle giving a few extra sniffs, peering around and frowning slightly. What was her friend up to?

As they settled around their favorite picnic table, Glitter felt a big smile stretch across her snout. She loved school, but it was always nice to have some free time to woof and joke with her friends!

"Did you see when Scooter tried to make his shifting magic big this morning?" Sparkle asked, wide-eyed. "He sent Flip flying across the room so fast, he tumbled snout over paws into a bookshelf!"

Twinkle clapped a paw over her eyes. "Barking bulldogs, what a disaster!"

The pups barked excitedly about their

morning lessons while they ate. Glitter munched on her peanut butter sandwich and carrot sticks, quietly listening to her friends. Sometimes she just liked to sit back and take everything in. She wasn't as outgoing as Sparkle, or as boisterous as Flash, or as opinionated as Twinkle, but that was what made their friendships special! They each brought something different to the group, the same way they each had their own unique magical skills.

Suddenly, she noticed Sparkle gazing out into the distance. Sparkle had an odd look on her golden snout.

"What is it?" Glitter asked gently.

Sparkle pointed a paw. "Check out those clouds!" She frowned. "They're looking ruff."

Glitter turned to look behind her and immediately spotted a pupload of dark, menacing clouds hanging low over the water. From their position up on Howl Hill, the pups had a sweeping view to sea. She frowned. "Bow wow, those don't look good."

Lightning flickered far out in the distance, crackling across the dark sky. The trees in the courtyard began to sway and rustle in the breeze.

"Whoa!" Glitter yelped, watching as her lunch bag blew right off the table and across the courtyard.

Before Glitter could shake a paw, Flash was racing after the bag. "Rescue missionnnnn!" she yipped dramatically. Glitter couldn't help giggling. She clapped her paws as Flash

returned with the lunch bag hanging from her mouth.

"I think it's time to head back inside," Sparkle said quietly, packing up her things. Glitter noticed her friend's golden horn sparkling faintly. She would bet that Sparkle's feeling magic was telling her that the storm was headed their way!

The four friends gathered their lunches.

All around them, other pups were doing the same. The wind was getting stronger and gustier by the minute, even though the clouds were still far out to sea. It was a warm day, but Glitter shivered in the blustery air. Brrr!

As the pups set paw back inside Cutiecorn Academy, Mrs. Horne and some other teachers met them in the hallway. Mrs. Horne held up a paw for quiet, and everyone immediately stopped their barking.

"I'm sure you've all noticed that the weather has taken a fur-raising turn," she announced calmly. "It appears that a big storm is rolling in. We're going to dismiss you early today so that everyone can get home safely."

The hallway erupted in barks and cheers. Early dismissal? Furbulous!

Mrs. Horne smiled patiently. "It's always exciting to have the afternoon free, but it's important to remember that this is for your own safety. Now, let's all get our paws in gear! Please gather your things and head straight home."

Pups of all ages scattered along the hallway, packing up their backpacks and yipping with their friends. Flash did a little backflip, and even Twinkle wore a smile on her snout. But Glitter had a strange feeling in her belly. She couldn't quite put a paw on it. Was it just that she'd always been nervous around lightning? Was she disappointed to miss their afternoon lessons? Was she worried that her mom's flowers might be uprooted by the storm?

No, this was something different . . . but what? It was just a storm, right?

Chapter 5

Things were already looking very different when Glitter stepped back outside Cutiecorn Academy with her friends. The dark clouds were much closer now, and moving impawsibly fast.

"Flying fur balls, we were only inside for a few minutes!" Flash cried.

Twinkle frowned. "This storm is no joke. Let's shake a tail, pups."

"I really don't like thunder," Sparkle said suddenly, so quietly that they could barely hear her.

Glitter wrapped her friend in a hug. She could feel that Sparkle was shaking. "We'll be with you the whole time," she said.

Cutiecorns were streaming out of the school now, some heading up Howl Hill and others down toward Barking Bay. Woofs and yelps filled the air as some pups pointed excitedly at the darkening sky. Other pups looked skittish, moving quickly on their paws. Their eyes darted up to the sky. Glitter knew that, like Sparkle, a lot of Cutiecorns were afraid of thunder. The noise could be truly fur-raising!

Glitter, Sparkle, Flash, and Twinkle trotted

up the hill, eager to get home before the rain began. The sky overhead was still a brilliant blue, but they knew it wouldn't last long.

A gust of wind came up behind them, causing all four pups to yelp in surprise. Flash, the smallest of the friends, tumbled forward, paws over snout!

"Hot dog!" she barked, standing up and brushing off her fur. "I'm glad this wind is at our backs. I'm just going to let it push me all the way home!"

"Should we add some rocks to your backpack to weigh you down?" Twinkle suggested with a wink.

"Bow wow, what's happening down there?" Sparkle asked suddenly. She pointed a paw at the boat docks near the base of Howl Hill.

The docks were full of Cutiecorns! They were moving fast on their paws, securing and covering all the boats. Others were hauling in sandbags to place along the shoreline. Glitter knew that lots of rain could cause the water in the bay to rise quickly. It was important to keep the island from flooding!

"All paws on deck!" a familiar voice barked from below.

Flash jumped to her paws. "Hey, that's my dad!"

Glitter glanced at her friends. "Should we go lend a paw?"

"Fur sure!" Flash yipped, racing down the hill before her friends could even blink.

Glitter, Twinkle, and Sparkle looked at one another. Glitter's eyes lingered on Sparkle, who paused, then nodded firmly in agreement. "Are you sure?" Glitter asked.

"Friends stick together!" Sparkle said bravely, breaking into a run.

Running after her friends, Glitter couldn't help giggling a little. Flash never wasted a moment!

"I'm not so sure about this," Twinkle muttered, racing along next to her. "Mrs. Horne said to go straight home."

"Don't worry, Twinkle," Glitter said with a sweet smile. "Let's just see if we can help Flash's dad for a few minutes. We'll head home before the clouds reach the island. Pup's honor!"

Glitter couldn't deny it—she always wanted to help a pup in need. She knew it was important to stay safe and be smart. But she felt confident that they could help out and still get home before the storm rolled in!

By the time Glitter, Twinkle, and Sparkle caught up with Flash, she was already helping her dad pull the boat back over to the dock.

They all tossed their backpacks down and grabbed a rope. In no time, Flash's dad had tied it down tightly.

"That was so much easier with all the extra paws," he said with a grin. "Thanks, pups!"

"How else can we help?" Glitter asked, glancing up at the sky. They still had time!

Flash's dad ruffled her fur. "Glitter, you would do just about anything for anyone, wouldn't you?"

Glitter blushed as Flash's dad went on. "You pups have already done enough. Now you need to head home and get safe before those clouds come much closer." He grabbed a thick rope in his paws. "I'm just going to tie the boat to an extra mooring, and then I'll be right behind you."

The four friends picked up their backpacks, pausing to hoist them onto their backs. Only then did Glitter really take in all of the commotion around the docks! Even more grown-up Cutiecorns had arrived in the last few minutes. They'd created a long line, passing sandbags from paw to paw and piling them along the shore. Glancing to one side, Glitter could see similar preparations happening all the way down toward Barking Bay. Some Cutiecorns were even using their magic to move sandbags through the air!

"Bye, Dad!" Flash called, waving a paw.

But just as the pups began trotting up the hill again, a sharp bark rang out and stopped them in their tracks.

"Help!"

Glitter and her friends whirled around, looking for the source of the bark. It was a French Bulldog, racing back from the end of one of the docks. His eyes were wide with panic.

Flash's dad and some other pups put up their paws to stop him. "What's wrong?" a Sheepdog asked.

The French Bulldog could barely catch his breath. "My fishing boat is missing—and so is my son."

The grown-ups began woofing a million questions all at once. Glitter could hardly make sense of what they were saying, but she didn't need to. The heavy, sinking feeling in the pit of her stomach told her everything she needed to know.

"Glitter, are you okay?" Twinkle asked, watching her carefully.

"I think I know what pup they're barking about," Glitter said quietly. "It's Batty . . . Batty is missing!"

Chapter 6

"Dad! Dad!" Flash yapped, racing through the crowd with her friends on her tail. When she reached her dad, Flash panted, "We know the missing pup!" She turned to the French Bulldog. "Is it Batty? Is he your son? We just met him yesterday."

The French Bulldog nodded, his eyes scanning the choppy water the whole time. "He's spent a lot of time at sea with me, and he's allowed to take my fishing boat out around the island. But he's never faced a storm like this on his own."

Just then, a rumble of thunder boomed through the air. Sparkle shuddered, squeezing her eyes shut. The wind gusted, and Glitter saw Twinkle quietly put a paw on Flash's shoulder to keep her from tumbling again.

Flash's dad glanced up at the sky. He seemed to be calculating something. Then he ran back to his boat and untied the cover as fast as his paws would go. "We can take my boat on patrol. There's still time before the storm moves overhead."

A Yellow Lab used her magic to untie

another boat across the dock. "I'll take a second crew. We can go in opposite directions. We'll cover more water that way."

While Glitter, Sparkle, Flash, and Twinkle watched, the grown-ups all sprang into action. Each boat suddenly had four or five aboard. Batty's dad jumped in with Flash's dad and some other Cutiecorns, helping release the boat from the mooring. Others raced down the shoreline on paw, hoping to catch sight of Batty and the fishing boat. A few of the grown-ups even used their magic to amplify their barks. Glitter could hear "Batty! Batty, where are you?" echoing up and down the coast.

"What can we do to help?" Flash called to her dad as his boat pulled away from the dock.

He waved a reassuring paw. "Head home now! Tell Mom and Dash where I've gone. We'll find Batty and be back in two shakes of a pup's tail."

The pups watched as the two boats headed out into the choppy water. Glitter felt icy cold from her ears down to her paws—and it wasn't from the wind.

"Poor Batty," she whispered as she and her friends headed up Howl Hill once again. "He must be scared out of his fur."

Sparkle nodded. "He couldn't have known this storm was coming. No one did!"

"I wish there was something else we could do," Glitter said with a sigh. She hated to turn her back when a friend needed help!

Twinkle gave her a hug. "You heard Flash's dad—they'll find Batty in no time. He's in great paws. The most important thing for us to do is get home safely."

The four friends trotted along in thoughtful silence, panting as they reached the top of the hill. Glitter glanced over her shoulder to see the dark clouds moving in over Barking Bay. Out at sea, sheets of rain had started to fall. Within minutes, the storm would cover all of Puppypaw Island!

"Hey, pups!" A bark rose over the wind. Glitter and her friends turned to see Fizzle and Frolic running up behind them.

"How do you like this storm? Ter-ruffically exciting, right?" Fizzle said with a grin.

Frolic rolled her eyes. "I keep telling Fizzle he won't like the storm so much once his fur is soaked and freezing. We've got to get home to Mom and Swirl before the rain hits!"

Glitter froze in her tracks. "And Pogo. Mom, Swirl, and Pogo are all at home, right?"

"Pogo should be home by now," Fizzle said with a shrug. "The last time I saw him, he was talking to that pup you told him about. What was his name? Flappy?"

Glitter felt her fur stand on end. She couldn't even bark.

Luckily, Flash spoke up. "You mean Batty?" Her eyes were wide as she looked from Fizzle to Glitter.

Fizzle nodded. "That's it. They must have hit it off, because we didn't see them again for the rest of the morning."

Frolic was watching Glitter, Flash, Twinkle, and Sparkle closely. The four friends hadn't moved a paw. "What's wrong?" Frolic asked. "I'm sure Pogo and Batty are both home. There's nothing to worry about."

Glitter swallowed hard. She felt her eyes fill with tears. Bow wow, she couldn't start crying now! That would only frighten Fizzle and Frolic. She stood up tall, determined to be brave.

"Batty took his dad's fishing boat out before the storm. He hasn't come back yet." Glitter's voice shook. She watched as understanding dawned on her brother's and sister's faces. Their jaws dropped.

"And I think Pogo is with him."

Chapter 7

Fizzle and Frolic erupted in a flurry of barks.

"Where did they go?"

"He's not a good swimmer!"

"Flying fur balls, we have to help him!"

Glitter stood quietly, thinking hard. She knew she had to take charge, and there was only one way to do it—with her magic. She closed her eyes. Slowly, slowly, she felt her caring magic rise up inside her. Her fur tingled.

"The best thing for you two to do is get home and be safe." Fizzle and Frolic began to protest, but Glitter held up a paw. "Pogo is already missing. Mom and Dad don't need you two to be lost in the storm. They must be worried sick already." She used all the caring magic she could muster to help her brother and sister understand. They needed to be safe, and she had to focus on Pogo and Batty. She couldn't protect them, too!

Fizzle's and Frolic's faces both fell. "You're right," Frolic said quietly. "We have to get home."

"Tell Mom and Dad what's going on," Glitter instructed. "Let them know that

Flash's dad and a bunch of other grown-ups are already out looking for Batty and Pogo." She glanced around at her friends, and suddenly she had an idea.

"You're not coming with us?" Fizzle yelped. "But, Glitter, it's too dangerous!"

Glitter gave her brother a hug. "I promise I'll be careful. But I think I can help."

Fizzle and Frolic raced up the lane toward home. As they disappeared around a corner and out of sight, a light rain started to fall.

"There's no time to lose," Twinkle said, all business. "This rain is going to start coming down harder and harder."

Glitter looked around at her friends. "Listen, Pogo is my little brother. I can't go home when

I know he's missing. But I don't want to put you three in danger. You don't have to—"

"You're barking up the wrong tree, Glitter," Sparkle said bravely, holding up a paw. "Best friends stick together, especially when things get ruff. We're here to help you."

Glitter took a deep breath. Her friends

were the grrrreatest, paws down! She had an idea about how to track down Batty and Pogo, but she would need all of her friends' magic in order to make it work. "Right. Here's the plan." She turned to Sparkle. "Sparkle, I think we need your feeling magic. Can you use it to seek out the pups?"

Sparkle's eyes grew big and round. She nodded, looking uncertain.

Glitter put a paw on her friend's shoulder. "I know you're scared. And I know it's a lot to ask. You're going to have to make your magic big, since we have no idea how far away Batty and Pogo might be." Glitter smiled, feeling her caring magic surge. "But I also know you can do it. You have the most pawsome feeling magic of any pup I know."

Sparkle grinned, looking more calm and confident with every word Glitter barked. She trotted over to the side of Howl Hill overlooking the docks, and her friends followed closely.

As Sparkle shut her eyes to find her magic, Glitter put a paw on her shoulder again. "You've got this," she whispered.

Sparkle's golden horn began to shimmer,

just a little at first, then brighter. Glitter, Flash, and Twinkle all held their breath. Glitter could feel Sparkle trembling with the effort of making her magic bigger and bigger.

Sparkle's eyes popped open. "Follow me!" she barked, racing down the hill before her friends even realized what was happening. They ran as fast as their paws would take them after her, ears flapping in the wind. The rain pelted their faces, and Glitter could feel her fur getting wet and heavy.

Sparkle reached the docks, turned right, and kept going—away from the beaches and toward the Canine Cliffs. Her horn gleamed brightly in the darkness, leading the way.

Glitter hadn't spent much time on this part of the island. She didn't know her way around, but she knew that she could trust Sparkle.

The coastline grew rocky, and soon the pups were scrambling over rocks as big as their snouts. "Almost there," Sparkle woofed over her shoulder. "Be careful. These rocks are slippery!"

Glitter peered every which way, trying to spot any sign of Batty or Pogo. The rain was coming down so heavily now that it was hard to see her own paws in front of her snout. Thunder boomed, and Glitter felt a shiver run through her soggy fur.

"There!" Sparkle stopped on top of a big rock, pointing a paw out at the water. A little fishing boat bobbed wildly on the waves. Glitter felt her heart leap . . .

But the boat was empty.

Flash darted to the water's edge. "The boat's rope is looped around this big rock here, see? They tied it here on purpose."

"Smart pups," Twinkle barked. "I'll bet they got out of the water when they saw the storm rolling in, even though they didn't have time to get back to the dock." She pointed a paw. "There are two life vests here, too, so we know Batty and Pogo were *both* on the boat."

Glitter was relieved, but it only lasted a moment. Then she looked left and right down the rocky beach. There wasn't a building in sight, just rocks and cliffs and swaying pines. The wind whipped through her fur.

She looked at her friends, who were all soaked and shivering. "So if they're not with the boat . . . where are they?"

Chapter 8

Sparkle shook the rain from her fur and frowned. "I'm beat, pups! I want to use my magic to keep searching for Batty and Pogo, but I just don't know if I have it in me." She sat down heavily, looking sad.

Twinkle put a reassuring paw on her friend's shoulder. "Don't worry, Sparkle. You've done more than enough. Let me take a turn!"

Twinkle stood very still, letting the rain pelt her fur. "Where would the pups have gone for shelter?" she muttered under her breath. Her blue horn began to glow, only a little at first, then brighter and brighter. She looked up and down the coastline, letting her seeing magic guide her.

Glitter watched her friend carefully. Twinkle was especially good at using her magic to solve riddles and problems. Figuring out where Batty and Pogo had gone would be her biggest riddle yet!

After a moment, Twinkle began trotting farther down the rocky shore. She didn't bark a word, and her friends followed silently. The air was filled with the occasional rumble of thunder overhead, the sound of waves crashing on the rocks, and the wind whipping through the pine trees, plus the steady patter of rain.

The pups moved farther from the water, scrambling up closer to the rocky cliff face. Twinkle's glowing horn acted almost as a flashlight, shining through the heavy rain. She turned this way and that. Glitter didn't know what her friend was looking for, but she was definitely searching for something specific.

"There!" Twinkle's bark cut through the air, making the rest of the pups jump in surprise.

"You scared us out of our fur!" Flash yipped, giggling nervously. "There . . . where?"

Twinkle pointed a paw, and her friends all

looked excitedly, expecting to see Batty and Pogo. Glitter's heart leaped. Were they okay?

Glitter couldn't see much of anything at all—definitely no pups.

But wait! She could hear something!

Very faint barks rang through the air. Bow wow, they were coming from right where Twinkle had pointed!

Glitter woofed in excitement. "Barking bulldogs, is that them?"

Twinkle nodded, wiping the rain from her eyes with one paw.

Flash ran around in excited circles, but Sparkle looked confused. "Where are they? I hear the barking, but I still don't see any sign of them."

"Follow me," Twinkle said. She led her friends closer to the bottom of the cliffs, until they were right up next to the rock face. Glitter could hear the frightened barks more clearly now . . . but where were they coming from?

Twinkle stopped next to an enormous pine tree. One of the biggest branches had cracked and fallen in the wind. It lay across the ground at the base of the cliff. "Look closely," Twinkle barked. "There's a cave in the rock!"

The pups all peered through the driving rain, unsure of what they were seeing.

Hot dog, Twinkle was right! There was a small opening in the rock just behind the fallen tree branch. They could barely make it out—the opening was almost entirely blocked by the giant branch.

"Pogo! Batty!" Glitter woofed as loud as she could. "Are you in there?"

She felt her heart pound as she waited for a response.

"Yes!" came her little brother's bark a second later. "But we're stuck—we can't get past that branch!"

Flash whooped and did a backflip in the air. "They're safe! We found them!"

Glitter felt a huge grin stretch across her snout. It was a pawsome relief to hear Pogo's familiar bark. But she knew that none of them were safe yet. The storm was raging, and other branches could come down at any minute.

"Flash, it's your turn," Glitter said, turning

to her smallest friend. "We need to get them out of there right away. Can you use your shifting magic to move the tree branch?"

Flash stopped celebrating at once. Her eyes grew wide. "I've never moved anything that big before."

"I know," Glitter said gently. "But I also know that you can do it. You may be small, but you have the biggest magic of any pup I know. Make your magic big, Flash!"

A confident smile lit up Flash's snout. "Let's do this," she said, facing the fallen branch. Her purple horn began to glow.

Glitter, Sparkle, and Twinkle all held their breath, watching their friend work her magic. "You can do it," Glitter whispered over and over again. "You can do it!"

The giant tree branch moved ever so slightly. At first, Glitter thought she might have imagined it. But then, slowly, slowly, slowly, the branch creaked and shifted off the ground. Inch by inch, it moved through the air until the pups could see the small cave entrance. Flash used her magic to set the

branch gently back on the ground, off to one side. As she did, two pups came bursting out of the cave.

"Pogo!" Glitter barked, wrapping her brother in a tremendous hug. "I was so worried about you!"

Pogo sighed in relief. "I knew you'd find us," he said.

Glitter turned to Batty, who was surrounded by Twinkle, Sparkle, and Flash. "Are you okay?"

Batty gave a small smile. "I'm ter-ruff-ic now! The storm snuck up on us, and we didn't have time to get back to the dock." He paused, hanging his snout. "I'm so sorry we made you worry."

"We're just glad to see you," Glitter said, giving Batty a hug.

A bolt of lightning cut across the sky, and Twinkle cleared her throat. "Listen up, pups— we're not out of harm's way yet. We need to get home, and fast!"

Chapter 9

"Ready, everyone?" Glitter looked at her friends through the driving rain. She felt her pink horn glinting in the gloom. She'd need all her caring magic to protect the group from harm until they could get to safety!

They'd woofed about taking shelter in the cave all together, since the entrance was clear again. But the tide was coming in, bringing the raging waters closer every minute. Glitter also knew that the grown-ups wouldn't give up looking for Batty and Pogo until they had been found. It wasn't safe for anyone to be on the water right now! The pups had to get back so that everyone knew that they were okay—and the sooner the better!

The other five pups nodded, serious and determined.

"Stay right on my tail!" Glitter instructed, racing off along the rocks again. She ran close to the cliff face this time, using it as shelter from the wind. She could hear her friends panting behind her. She made sure not to go so fast that Pogo and Batty couldn't keep up!

Batty's dad's fishing boat was still bobbing up and down on the choppy waves. "I'm gonna be in so much trouble," Glitter heard Batty mutter to himself as they dashed by.

After what seemed like forever, they reached the base of Howl Hill again. Glitter paused on her paws to catch her breath. Her friends skidded to a stop beside her. No sooner had they stopped than a huge clap of thunder boomed through the air.

"Bow wow!" Pogo cried, grabbing on to Glitter. Flash jumped so high in surprise that she almost did a backflip!

Twinkle squinted up the hill through the rain. "It's still a long way home from here, pups. The wind and rain are even worse up high on the hill."

"I don't think this storm is blowing over anytime soon," Sparkle added, glancing off toward the horizon.

Glitter thought for a moment, feeling her caring magic flow through her. What was the best way to keep her friends safe?

"I think we should head for Barking Bay," she said finally. "It's not far, and there are plenty of places there where we can wait out the storm."

Glitter glanced around at the five other pups, who all nodded slowly.

"That makes puptastic sense," Flash barked. She leaped to her feet and shook the rain from her fur. "Lead the way, Glitter!"

Glitter turned away from Howl Hill and looked toward Barking Bay. She could see the buildings off in the distance, specks of bright color under a canopy of dark clouds. Just before getting her paws in gear to run again, she glanced at the docks to her right.

Her heart sank.

"Uh-oh," she said quietly.

Pogo appeared at her shoulder. "What's wrong?"

Glitter pointed a paw. "Flash, your dad's boat isn't back yet. The other one they took to search for Batty is docked, but your dad's boat is still gone."

Flash's eyes grew wide. For once, she had nothing to bark.

Batty clapped a paw over his mouth. "This is all my fault," he said quietly.

"No one knew this storm was coming," Glitter said, feeling her caring magic surge as she turned to Batty. "You did the right thing, getting out of the water and finding a place to wait it out."

"Do you think the grown-ups are in trouble?" Sparkle woofed with concern.

"Don't forget, they all have powerful magic," Twinkle said. "I'm sure they're okay, even in this fur-raising situation."

Glitter had a funny feeling in her belly again. As usual, she couldn't put a paw on it, but she also couldn't ignore it.

"I have an idea," she said quietly, and five pairs of eyes turned to look at her. "But it will only work if you all agree to go ahead without me."

Sparkle, Twinkle, Flash, Pogo, and Batty began barking at once.

"No way!"

"Are you out of your fur?"

"No pup left behind!"

Glitter smiled. "I know it sounds crazy. I promise I'm not out of my fur. But I have an idea, and I need to make my caring magic as big as possible for it to work." She paused. "I can't do that if I'm using my magic to protect all of you out here."

Understanding dawned on her friends' faces. "You're always one pawstep ahead of us, aren't you?" Twinkle said gruffly, giving her a hug. "I'll take the lead. Let's go, pups!"

Pogo gave Glitter a kiss on the cheek. "I love you, big sister."

"Love you more," Glitter said with a wink. "Now go on—I'll be right on your tail."

As she watched her friends race off toward Barking Bay, Glitter felt a shiver run through her fur. Now she was all alone in the storm, with only a pawfectly crazy idea to guide her.

"Might as well give it a try," she barked under her breath.

Glitter walked carefully out to the very end of the dock. Wind whipped through her fur, and waves splashed up over her paws. The rain was coming down so hard that it felt like hundreds of little pinpricks on her skin. Glitter took a deep breath, stood perfectly still . . . and tuned it all out.

She focused on feeling her magic, then growing it bigger and bigger. She'd never felt her magic this strongly before! She could see the glow from her horn lighting up the air all

around her, cutting through the rain. It was working! She could only hope her magic was big enough to protect the grown-ups out on the water . . . wherever they were.

Glitter let the magic course through her, determined to keep it big for as long as she could. Just then, she saw a faint light out in the water. Was it a reflection? Were her eyes playing tricks on her?

"There it is!" A bark cut through the storm, and the light inched closer.

Glitter squinted through the darkness. She could see an outline on the water. Could it be?

Yes! It was Flash's dad's boat! And there was Flash's dad at the helm, waving a paw as he steered toward the dock.

"Is that you, Glitter?" he barked.

Glitter waved back, finally letting her magic go. She took a deep breath, exhausted. But she couldn't help the smile stretching across her snout. "Yes, it's me! You're okay!"

Flash's dad threw a rope around the dock mooring and leaped out. "Thanks to you," he woofed with a grin. "It was so dark out on the

water that we couldn't see our paws in front of our snouts. Even with all of our magic, we had no idea which way to go to get back to the island."

"We're lucky you were here, young pup." Batty's dad set paw on the dock. "That's some puptastic magic you have there." He smiled, but Glitter could still see the worry in his eyes. He hadn't found Batty or his boat.

Glitter beamed, feeling a sudden surge of energy. "You're not the only ones who are back safe on Puppypaw Island." Batty's dad's eyes lit up. "I know someone who is going to be pawsomely excited to see you!"

Chapter 10

"Wait up, Flash!" Glitter giggled, racing down the beach after her friend. "I can't move driftwood that fast!"

Flash turned back, bouncing on her paws. "You're doing ter-ruff-ically well, Glitter! Just concentrate."

Glitter and her friends, along with lots of other Cutiecorns, were down on the beach, cleaning up from the storm. They had spent the rest of yesterday waiting out the storm in the Pupcorn Parlor, where Batty and Flash happily reunited with their dads. Mr. Puggypop, the owner of the Pupcorn Parlor, had given them all huge buckets of popcorn to snack on while they waited for the storm to pass. It had been such a relief to be safe,

warm, dry, and surrounded by friends!

Today, Mrs. Horne had canceled school so all the pups could lend a paw to the clean-up efforts around Puppypaw Island. Flash had taken the lead, helping her friends practice their shifting magic by moving hunks of driftwood into a pile.

Twinkle trotted up, carrying a big piece of driftwood in her teeth. She dropped it at Flash's feet. "I just spent fifteen minutes moving one tiny piece of wood with my magic," she grumbled. "I think it's probably better for everyone if I do this the old-fashioned way."

Glitter laughed. She had to agree with Twinkle! This was a good way for them to practice their magic, sure, but Flash had stacked whole piles of wood in the time the rest of them had each moved a piece or two.

"No matter how long it takes us to move the driftwood, this beach is going to be back in tip-top shape in the shake of a tail," Sparkle said, appearing at Twinkle's side.

Glancing up and down the beach, Glitter couldn't keep a smile from her snout. Cutiecorns were spread out as far as she could see! They piled up driftwood, removed sandbags, gathered garbage that had been strewn by the wind, and raked out the wet sand. Some pups used their magic, while others worked by paw. The air was filled with cheerful barks and laughter. There was even music playing! Glitter's heart swelled. She loved this island— and the Cutiecorns who called it home!

Glitter stepped over to a small piece of

driftwood. She stared at it, trying to tune out the noise and bustle around her. It was much harder to tap into her shifting magic than her caring magic. Caring magic came so naturally to her! But she was determined to keep practicing. Slowly, the wood rose off the sand. It danced through the air as Glitter concentrated on it with all her might. Finally, she used her magic to lower it gently on top of the driftwood pile. Bow wow—that was ruff work!

"Puptastic job, Glitter!" a familiar voice called. "I love to see that focus and determination!" Mrs. Horne walked down the beach toward them, her gray-and-white fur shining in the morning sunlight.

Glitter blushed. She hadn't expected anyone to be watching her!

"Hi, Mrs. Horne!" Sparkle barked, waving a paw. Flash raced to the teacher's side, and Twinkle walked over with a shy smile.

"I heard you four were working down here," Mrs. Horne began, "and I was hoping to have a quick bark with you. Rumor has it that you had quite the adventure yesterday after leaving school."

Glitter shared a look with her friends. Barking bulldogs, were they in trouble? They were supposed to go straight home after school!

Mrs. Horne put a paw on Glitter's shoulder. "Don't worry," she said kindly. "Batty and Pogo made it home safely because of the four of you. You all used your magic to be caring, thoughtful, and brave. You should be proud—I certainly am!"

Smiles spread across the snouts of all four pups. Twinkle blushed, which made Glitter smile even wider.

"Above all," Mrs. Horne continued, "the four of you were able to make your magic big, even in the most serious of situations. And that was because you had big hearts behind it! So . . ." She held out a paw to reveal four glimmering golden heart charms. "These are for your bracelets, one for each of you. You've earned them!"

"Bow wow, thank you!" Glitter and her friends all woofed in surprise. Mrs. Horne attached their new charms to each of their bracelets. Glitter held up her paw and admired the heart, sparkling in the sunlight. Her own heart swelled with pride.

"Keep up the good work, pups!" Mrs. Horne said, glancing over at the pile of driftwood. She gave them a funny little salute as she walked on across the beach.

Twinkle flopped down on the sand as soon as Mrs. Horne was out of earshot. "Hot dog, I don't believe it! At first, I thought we were in a pupload of trouble!"

Glitter, Sparkle, and Flash sat down next to her, laughing.

"We're a pretty pawsome team," Glitter said, looking around at her friends.

"Speaking of teams," Sparkle woofed with a gleam in her eye. "When we're done cleaning up here, Twinkle and I challenge you to a beach volleyball rematch."

Flash leaped to her paws and began racing circles around them. "A rematch? Bring it on! Glitter and I will be the volleyball victors yet again!"

Twinkle rolled her eyes, then looked at Sparkle with a sly grin. "Maybe we'd better find Batty again. I have a feeling we're going to need his help!"

About the Author

Shannon Penney doesn't have any magical powers,
but she has ter-ruff-ic fun writing about them! If she
were a Cutiecorn, she'd have a turquoise horn and
the ability to turn everything into ice cream. For now,
she'll settle for the ice and snow of New Hampshire,
where she writes, edits, and goes on adventures with
her husband, two kids, and two non-magical cats.

DON'T MISS THE CUTIECORNS' NEXT
ADVENTURE: CARNIVAL CHAOS

Chapter 1

"Bow wow, Sparkle, that was puptastic!" Twinkle cheered, clapping her paws. On either side of her, her friends Glitter and Flash barked and whooped in agreement.

Up onstage, Sparkle took a graceful bow. Her golden fur shimmered in the spotlight— and so did the golden horn between her ears. After all, Sparkle, Twinkle, and their friends weren't regular puppies. They were Cutiecorns! The colorful horns on their heads gave them pawsome magical powers. But Sparkle had just wowed them with no magic at all!

"I had no idea you could sing like that!" Glitter said, giving Sparkle a hug as she stepped down from the stage.

"Me neither," Flash barked, racing in excited circles. "That was incrediwoof!"

Sparkle blushed, but a happy smile stretched across her snout. "Thanks! I've been practicing doggone hard."

"This talent show is going to be the best thing Puppypaw Island has ever seen!" Flash cried. "Just think how impressed our visitors will be!"

Twinkle couldn't help grinning at her

friend's enthusiasm. Flash never missed an opportunity to yap on and on about something! Even though Twinkle pretended to be grumpy about it sometimes, it was one of the things she liked best about the little Yorkshire Terrier—she was a bundle of energy and excitement! Plus, the talent show was definitely something to bark about.

"It *is* pretty ter-ruff-ic that we get to host Cutiecorns from far and wide this weekend," Twinkle said with a nod.

Sparkle danced on her paws. "Yup, turns out something good did come from those mischievous little kittens who showed up here! Everyone wants to get to know one another a little better," she said. "The first-ever Cutiecorn

Carnival and Talent Show is going to be a grrrrrreat success. I just know it!"

Twinkle peered around the auditorium from her seat in the first row. In front of her was an impressive stage with heavy red curtains and bright lights. Behind her, rows of padded seats stretched on and on into the darkness. Of all the rooms at the pups' school, Cutiecorn Academy, Twinkle thought this one must be the grandest. It was nice of Mrs. Horne, the head of the school, to let them stay after and practice on the big stage!

"My turn," Glitter said quietly, climbing up the steps. She cued some music, took a deep breath, and began dancing, twirling, and leaping across the stage. Twinkle knew that her friend had been taking ballet lessons ever since she was a little pup, but she'd had no idea that Glitter had turned into such a barking good ballerina!

Sparkle and Flash both looked at Twinkle with wide eyes. They were surprised, too!

When the music faded, Glitter posed pawfectly still for a moment. Then she curtsied as her friends erupted into a flurry of barks and cheers.

"You're so graceful!"

"Hot dog, what a performance!"

"You're a puptastic ballerina!"

This time, it was Glitter's turn to blush as she stepped down from the stage. "I love to dance," she said with a happy sigh. "It's my favorite thing in the whole world!"